The Witch's Christmas

Story and pictures by NORMAN BRIDWELL

SCHOLASTIC INC.
New York Toronto London Auckland Sydney

For Nicholas and Benjamin

0-590-40434-2

Copyright © 1986, 1970 by Norman Bridwell.
All rights reserved. Published by Scholastic Inc.

12 11 10 9 8 7 6 5 4 3 2 1   10   6 7 8 9/8 0 1/9
Printed in the U.S.A.   24

Halloween is very special for my brother and me —

— because we have a witch living next door.
She's our friend.

So we always have the best pumpkin
on our street.

When you have a witch for a friend
Christmas is very special, too.
When Christmas is near and it begins to snow,

our witch has very special snow at her house —

— and a very special snowman.

And sledding is more fun
with a witch on your sled.

Last year our witch went with us
to pick a Christmas tree, but —

— a tree picked us.
The tree wasn't very big.
And it wasn't very pretty.
But the witch said it was a special tree —

— and it was.

When we got the tree home,
it seemed to be prettier.
Bigger, too.

Her own tree was pretty, but a little different.

And she had a lovely wreath on her door.

When we saw her gifts being wrapped,
it made me think of the Christmas shopping
I had to do.

But shopping was easy with the witch
helping me.

Our witch went Christmas caroling
with a few friends.

But no one came to sing at her door —
except my brother and me.

On Christmas Eve we went to sleep, but our witch was waiting for Santa Claus.

Where was Santa?
Something must have happened to him.

She jumped on her broom and set off
to find him. She flew very high.

Her witch's nose led her straight to Santa.
Santa had run into a spaceship and his
reindeer were all tangled up.

The spaceman said the accident
had knocked out the ship's controls.
They couldn't get down.

Santa's sled was too badly damaged to fly.
The witch had an idea. She put a spell
on her magic broom.

It became many magic brooms.

There was a broom for everyone.

Our witch led them right to our house.

Santa gave us our toys, and —

— we had a midnight Christmas party
before Santa had to fly away on his
broom to finish his deliveries.

What else could you want if you had
a Merry Christmas witch like ours?